A
HEART'S
*P*ROMISE

ALSO BY COLLEEN COBLE

ACCLAIM FOR COLLEEN COBLE

"Coble's atmospheric and suspenseful series launch should appeal to fans of Tracie Peterson and other authors of Christian romantic suspense."

—*Library Journal* review of
Tidewater Inn

"Romantically tense, but with just the right touch of danger, this cowboy love story is surprisingly clever—and pleasingly sweet."

—USAToday.com review of
Blue Moon Promise

"Colleen Coble will keep you glued to each page as she shows you the beauty of God's most primitive land and the dangers it hides."

—www.RomanceJunkies.com

"[An] outstanding, completely engaging tale that will have you on the edge of your seat . . . A must-have for all fans of romantic suspense!"

—TheRomanceReadersConnec-
tion.com review of *Anathema*

"Colleen Coble lays an intricate trail in *Without a Trace* and draws the reader on like a hound with a scent."

—*Romantic Times*, 4½ stars

"Coble's historical series just keeps getting better with each entry."

—*Library Journal* starred review of
The Lightkeeper's Ball

"Don't ever mistake [Coble's] for the fluffy romances with a little bit of suspense. She writes solid suspense, and she ties it all together beautifully with a wonderful message."

—LifeinReviewBlog.com
review of *Lonestar Angel*

"This book has everything I enjoy: mystery, romance, and suspense. The characters are likable, understandable, and I can relate to them."

—TheFriendlyBookNook.com

"[M]ystery, danger, and intrigue as well as romance, love, and subtle inspiration. *The Lightkeeper's Daughter* is a 'keeper.'"

—OnceUponaRomance.net

"Colleen is a master storyteller."

—Karen Kingsbury, bestselling
author of *Unlocked* and *Learning*

A
HEART'S
$\mathcal{P}$ROMISE

COLLEEN
COBLE

THOMAS NELSON
Since 1798

NASHVILLE   MEXICO CITY   RIO DE JANEIRO

Published in Nashville, Tennessee, by Thomas Nelson. Thomas Nelson is a registered trademark of HarperCollins Christian Publishing, Inc.

Thomas Nelson titles may be purchased in bulk for educational, business, fund-raising, or sales promotional use. For information, please e-mail SpecialMarkets@ThomasNelson.com.

Scripture quotations are from the King James Version.

Publisher's Note: This novel is a work of fiction. Names, characters, places, and incidents are either products of the author's imagination or used fictitiously. All characters are fictional, and any similarity to people living or dead is purely coincidental.

Library of Congress Cataloging-in-Publication Data

Coble, Colleen.
 A heart's promise / Colleen Coble.
 pages ; cm. -- (A journey of the heart ; 5)
 Summary: "A rival threatens Emmie's budding romance with Isaac. At Fort Laramie, soldier Isaac Liddle determines he will court and win Emmie Croftner's hand. Though courting seems improbable for a woman in her condition, Emmie begins to care deeply for Issac and chafes as Jessica Dubois sets her bonnet for him. When Jessica learns of Emmie's secret pregnancy, she blackmails her. With the Sioux Wars raging outside the safety of Fort Laramie, Emmie knows she cannot lose Isaac. But will he reject her -- and her child -- if he learns the truth?"-- Provided by publisher.
 ISBN 978-0-7180-3168-8 (softcover)
 1. Man-woman relationships--Fiction. 2. Triangles (Interpersonal relations)--Fiction. I. Title.
 PS3553.O2285H435 2015
 813'.54--dc23 2015001999

Printed in the United States of America

15 16 17 18 19 20 RRD 6 5 4 3 2 1

In memory of my brother Randy Rhoads, who taught me to love the mountains of Wyoming, and my grandparents Everett and Eileen Everroad, who loved me unconditionally. May you walk those heavenly mountains with joy.

A LETTER FROM THE AUTHOR

Dear Reader,

I can't tell you how excited I am to share this story with you! It's the first series I ever wrote, and it will always be special to me because writing was how I dealt with my brother Randy's death. You'll see a piece of my dear brother in Rand's character throughout this series. These six books were originally titled *Where Leads the Heart* and *Plains of Promise*. They haven't been available in print form for nearly ten years, so I'm thrilled to share them with you. I've made some massive changes to them, and I hope you enjoy these new, updated stories. This installment begins to show what Sarah faces in winning Rand back again.

When my brother Randy was killed in a freak lightning accident, I went to Wyoming to see where he had lived. As I stood on the parade ground at Fort Laramie, the idea for the first book dropped into my head. I went home excited to write it. It took a year to write, and I thought for sure there would be a bidding war on it! ☺ Not so much. It took six more years for a publisher to pick it up. But the wait was worth it!

This series seemed a good one to break up into a serialization model to introduce readers to my work. Even in my early stories, I had to have villains and danger lurking around the corner. ☺ I hope you enjoy this trip back in time with me.

E-mail me at colleen@colleencoble.com and let me know what you think!

Love,
Colleen

ONE

October 1866, Fort Phil Kearny,
Wyoming Territory

Pregnant and unmarried.

Emmie Croftner mulled her condition over as she lay snuggled in her quilts. The prairie wind howled around the tent, and snow drifted through the cracks in the tent and collected in piles around her.

She'd thought nothing could be worse than Monroe's death, then his *real* wife had shown up. This was infinitely worse.

She wasn't sure how her best friend's husband, Rand Campbell, would treat her after hearing the news, but over the days that followed Emmie had found that he treated her no differently than he always had. He was just as solicitous of her as he was of his wife, Sarah. He truly did not seem to mind the change in the bargain they'd struck.

Had he told Isaac Liddle? She thought it likely since Isaac hadn't stopped by as much as usual. She threw back the covers, and her bare feet landed in snow. She didn't care if he came by or not. All men were fickle at best and treacherous at worst. She'd been certain his interest wouldn't survive her devastating news.

"Emmie?" Rand's voice came from the other side of the tent. "Our permanent quarters in Officers' Row are ready to move into. I have some soldiers out here ready to transfer our belongings."

"Coming!" Emmie jerked her flannel nightgown over her head and quickly donned her wool dress and boots. She grabbed her cloak and buttoned it around her before lifting the flap on the tent and joining Sarah.

Already dressed for the blustery late-October weather at Fort Phil Kearny, Sarah turned with a bright smile. Her red-gold hair sprang free from its bun and circled her face. "I'll be so glad to get in a real house. No stepping in snow tomorrow morning."

Several soldiers sidled in with a shy glance at the women. They hefted crates to their shoulders and hauled them out of the tent. Emmie and Sarah followed them across the fort's parade ground to the sounds of the fort band practicing in the single officers' quarters. Emmie spared a glance toward the hills that rose around the little fort in a picturesque panorama.

The cold wind practically blew them into their new home. Emmie shut the door behind Sarah and turned to survey the cabin. It was similar in layout to what they'd left behind in Fort Laramie but smaller in size. The pine boards still oozed sap and smelled of newly milled lumber. The fresh plaster walls looked clean but stark, with no trim around the windows or floor. The kitchen was bare of accessories but serviceable and clean. Emmie was so glad to be out of the tent, she didn't care how it looked.

"It's plain, I know, but I'll knock together a dry sink and corner cupboard as soon as I can." Rand took off his hat, and the sunlight through the window gleamed on his brown hair.

The door opened and snow swirled through

it, then it was shut again. "Already done, partner." Isaac's mustache quivered above his grin as he set a sturdy sawhorse down against the wall. "Be right back." He stepped outside and returned with another one, which he placed a couple of feet away from the first. Then he brought in four rough wood planks and laid them over the sawhorses. "This is the very latest in Fort Phil's kitchen decor. All the best-dressed kitchens have one. And I have it on the best authority that it makes a dandy ironing board as well."

Sarah ran to hug him. "Isaac, you darling!"

His blue eyes danced above his reddened cheeks, and he winked at Emmie. "Don't I get a hug from you too?"

Heat rushed to Emmie's cheeks. He hadn't shown his face for days and now he showed up talking about hugs. "Maybe when we get the chairs." She flushed again when he laughed.

"I'll hold you to it," he chuckled as he walked away.

Emmie delighted in helping Sarah fix up their tiny home over the next few days. They begged some wool blankets from the quartermaster and tacked them together to make rugs for the parlor and bedroom floors as well as for the small area in the hall that was partitioned off for Emmie. Rand came in with a triumphant smile with his booty of blue gingham for curtains and tablecloths. With Sarah's little knick-knacks around, the place looked very homey. Several of the other ladies were very friendly and stopped by with invitations to tea and some small offerings of household items.

Emmie dried her hands on a towel and put the last plate away. "I think I'll go for a walk. The wind isn't blowing too hard for a change. I'm going crazy cooped up inside. Want to come along?"

Sarah shook her head. "I don't think so. Rand tore his britches on some cactus yesterday, and I promised I'd mend them. Why don't you ask Isaac or one of the other officers to escort you? Any of them would jump at the chance."

Emmie shied away from the thought of Isaac. "I don't mind going alone." She had tried to avoid him ever since he brought by the camp chairs for the kitchen while she was taking their laundry to Soapsuds Row two days ago. She hoped he'd forgotten all about her forward comment.

The sun was beginning to go down, and the reds and golds touched the tops of the hills around the fort. The cold evening air felt invigorating, but Emmie shivered as wolves howled outside the stockade. She wrapped her cloak more tightly around her as she strolled along the sawdust path in front of the officers' quarters. She decided to wander in the direction of the front of the stockade.

A tall figure came toward her. "Mind if I join you?"

She flinched back before she recognized Isaac's face. "There's really no need. I'm perfectly all right. I just wanted a walk." Her pulse quickened.

"I could use a chance to stretch my legs myself." He fell into step beside her. "Did you have someplace special in mind to go, or shall we just look in some windows?"

She chuckled in spite of herself, then glanced at him hesitantly. He probably wouldn't let her do what she planned. "I know Rand said to stay away from the stockade perimeter, but I wish I could climb up in the blockhouse and look out over the wall for just a minute. I'm so tired of seeing the same things day after day. I haven't been outside the confines of this fort in weeks."

Isaac was silent for a minute. Emmie shivered again as she heard a pack of wolves howl off to her right, but he relaxed at the sound. "Those are real wolves and not Indians. I guess it wouldn't hurt for just a minute. But you have to promise to get away from the wall the minute I say we have to leave."

"I promise." She resisted the urge to squeal from excitement. He was really going to take her.

Isaac led her past the hospital and warehouses and through the tangle of hayricks, shops, and quarters for wagon makers and saddlers. He stepped carefully and pointed out piles of manure and mud for her to avoid before stopping outside the blockhouse.

She'd seemed to withdraw the moment she saw him. Did she think her pregnancy would curb his interest? He loved kids, and he could love any child of Emmie's. How would she react if he told her that? Would she run from that much interest? He wasn't good at understanding women.

"Let me tell the soldiers on duty what we're doing." He climbed up and found Corporal Lengel watching the horizon. "Miss Croftner would like to see the moon on Little Piney River. You see any hostiles?"

The corporal's weathered face broke into a grin. "Nothing moving out there, Lieutenant. Want me to hang around and watch, or can you handle it?"

Isaac ignored the soldier's amusement. "I think I can take care of it. I'll go get her." Once he was away from Lengel, he couldn't hold back his grin as he rejoined Emmie.

She grabbed at the hood of her cloak as the wind blew it off her dark-brown hair. "What's so funny?"

"I told Corporal Lengel I wanted to show you the moon on the Little Piney River."

"He'll think—"

"Well, I had to give him some reason."

Emmie flushed. "I don't want anyone getting the wrong idea about you and me."

The finality in her tone erased his smile. Didn't she feel the same tug he did?

She looked away. "Rumors can run through the fort like a–a herd of thundering buffalo."

He snorted. "Like you've ever seen a herd of thundering buffalo." Taking her arm, he helped her onto the ladder. "Watch your step."

The corporal grinned knowingly as they brushed past him to get to the window. "Call when you're finished here, Lieutenant." He winked as he backed down the ladder.

Her cheeks went even redder. "Now see what you've done."

Isaac just laughed. Ignoring her outburst, he pointed out the window. "Look at the river." He watched her face as she looked out over the terrain.

The trees along the river sparkled as though they were made of diamonds. The moon glittered on their coating of heavy frost, and the iced-over river caught the shimmering reflection and bounced it back.

He pointed. "That way is some land I have my eye on."

"Land? Out here?" She shivered. "Where are you from originally?"

Something warmed in the region of his heart at the interest in her voice. "El Paso. There were four of us boys." Pain squeezed his chest. "When the Confederacy started forcing Texans into the army, I lit out to join the Cavalry. My pa was livid."

She touched his arm. "I'm sure he forgave you. You had to follow your principles."

He pressed his lips together. "I went to see him before I headed out here. Pa wouldn't let me in the house. Two of my brothers died fighting, and he thinks I should have been there to take care of them."

Her fingers tightened on his forearm. "I'm so sorry."

He placed his hand over hers. "That means a lot. I'm all right. I aim to get a ranch of my own. I'll raise racehorses some day."

"Out here?" She turned to look back at him, and her eyes were huge. "It's so dangerous." She leaned out the window.

Isaac clasped her arm and pulled her back. "Don't do that! There could be Sioux out there just waiting to put an arrow through your pretty head."

When he touched her, she fell back against him. The press of her small form against him spread warmth all through his body. He caught the scent of something sweet and flowery in her hair.

She straightened up and started to pull away, but he turned her to face him. "A real lady always pays her debts, you know."

"What do you mean?" She put one hand against his chest.

His voice went husky as he leaned closer. "I

distinctly remember you promising me a hug when I brought the kitchen chairs. It's been two days and I haven't gotten my hug yet. I think I'd better charge you a little interest."

He drew her closer and Emmie's eyes widened as he bent his head, but she didn't turn away. He smelled the warm scent of her skin as his lips found hers. At first she stood stiffly in his embrace, and her lips didn't respond. He gathered her closer as her lips softened beneath his, and one small hand slid up his chest.

The next instant, she gave a tiny gasp and pulled away. Her chest rose and fell and she was trembling. "That was more than a little interest."

"I think it was just perfect." He traced a finger along the curve of her cheek. "Just like you."

Her blue eyes were huge in her face, and her lower lip trembled. "I–I'd better get back." Her words were a whisper. "Sarah will be wondering about me."

He nodded and let her go. She kept a wary eye on him as she took one last look out the window, then hurried down the ladder. She didn't wait for him but struck off toward the officers' quarters.

He followed her quickly. "Wait up, Emmie. What are you so scared of? I won't hurt you."

"I–I don't want you to think I'm the sort of girl who dallies in the moonlight," she gulped, her voice nearly inaudible. "Just because I'm a widow–and–and pregnant doesn't mean I'm looking for someone to fill in for Monroe."

The warm softness he'd felt evaporated at once. "I never thought you were. That husband of yours must have been a piece of work for you to be so prickly, but you don't need to lump all of us men in the same pot of stew. I wouldn't want to do anything to dishonor you or my God."

Her head jerked up. "Don't you say anything about Monroe. You don't know anything about him."

"I know he must have hurt you badly. When you arrived at Fort Laramie, you were like a stray dog everyone had kicked too often. I left you alone to lick your wounds, but it's time for you to put the past behind you and get on with your life." He swept his arm expansively. "This is a new country out here. You can forget Indiana. You can make a new life for yourself."

"I am making a new life. It just doesn't include kisses in the moonlight with you or anyone else."

"Maybe I'm rushing you a little." Isaac stepped

back from her. "But I'll be here when you decide to quit living in the past." He turned and strode back toward the officers' quarters.

Emmie's throat burned with unshed tears as she mounted the steps to the Campbells' door. She just didn't want to be hurt again. Isaac was interested only because there weren't any other unmarried women here. If they were in Indiana, he wouldn't give her a second glance. She'd never felt she was a lovable person until Monroe came into her life. And after he'd done what he did, she was sure something was inherently wrong with her. No one had ever loved her for herself. Not even her family.

Sarah looked up as she came in. "Did you have a nice walk? Oh—" She broke off when she saw the look on Emmie's face. "What's wrong?"

"Nothing. I'm just tired." Emmie forced a smile to her face. She felt Sarah's probing eyes, but she refused to meet her gaze. "I think I'll turn in early. I'll see you in the morning." She fled to the meager haven of her curtained-off bedroom. Sarah wouldn't understand.

She'd like to see her marry Isaac and settle down next door. But that wasn't going to happen, she vowed as she slipped between the cold sheets. Men just couldn't be trusted. Underneath his exuberance and flattery, Monroe had been just like her brothers and father. Just as selfish and deceitful. Isaac was no different. He was just hiding it like Monroe had done.

TWO

The fort chapel was a small cabin with seats that were rough, backless benches oozing sap. A small stove in one corner of the room belched out smoke along with a little warmth. Emmie, Sarah, and Sarah's little brother, Joel, sat on the second row beside Amelia Campbell, who was married to Rand's brother Jacob.

All three women were pregnant. Amelia's beautiful face was a little bloated, though her blue eyes still smiled in spite of her discomfort. At about six months, Sarah glowed with a beautiful vitality in her green eyes. And Emmie just wanted to hide in bed until it was all over.

Emmie never attended church in Wabash other than an occasional wedding. Her pa didn't hold with religion, even though he bellowed out hymns when he was drunk. Emmie always wondered where he'd learned them. He never talked much about how he was raised and she never knew her grandparents. Her pa always said religion was a crutch for weak people, but Emmie thought the liquor was more of a crutch.

The chaplain, Reverend Howard, was a nervous young man with thin, pale hair and a straggly mustache. He read from Isaiah 43:1–2: "'Fear not: for I have redeemed thee, I have called thee by thy name; thou art mine. When thou passest through the waters, I will be with thee; and through the rivers, they shall not overflow thee: when thou walkest through the fire, thou shalt not be burned; neither shall the flame kindle upon thee.'"

He closed his large Bible and cleared his throat. "Though it seems we are compassed about by the enemy in this place, God tells us to fear not. He is with us and he will be our shield and comfort."

Emmie was drawn by the words. Was the

minister right? She glanced at the back of Isaac's head in the row in front of her. He leaned slightly forward in his seat as he listened intently. Did God really care about her in a personal way? She'd never doubted the existence of God, but in her mind, he was a powerful being who looked down on mere mortals with distant interest. Oh, he might deign to involve himself in the moving of nations and history, but he wasn't concerned with the small day-to-day heartbreaks of an ordinary person like her. But was he? Did he send her out here to such good friends as the Campbells because he loved her and cared for her? The thought was comforting, and she wished she could believe it.

As the service ended and they stood to leave, Isaac's eyes caught hers for just a moment. She looked away quickly as Frances Grummond called to them. She was glad for an excuse to turn away from Isaac's warm blue eyes. The look in his gaze threatened to upset all her plans to keep her distance.

"Yoohoo, Emmie." Frances waved at them from across the room. She was a petite brunette with softly rounded curves and a delightful Southern accent. She, too, was expecting a baby soon. Frances hurried over when she saw she had her attention. "I'm having tea at my house. Won't you all join me?"

Sarah smiled and clapped. "I've gotten so tired of those same four walls. What can I bring?"

"I have everything prepared. I know my lack of cooking prowess is legendary, but my husband has secured the services of Private Brown as cook. His scones are exemplary."

"Sounds lovely," Amelia said. "Our men are out on wood detail or guard duty. What time do you want us?"

"Oh, about three. Bring your mending or whatever and we'll have a fine time of chatting. Mrs. Horton is joining us also. Her husband is tending to an outbreak of colds on the fort." Frances hurried to rejoin her husband.

Isaac turned and caught her gaze. He started toward her, and Emmie quickly turned to catch Sarah's arm. "Let's go to Amelia's and I'll fix lunch while she rests."

The fierce wind whipped Emmie's cloak about as she fought to keep her balance in the gale. She kept a hand on her hat to prevent it from blowing away.

Sometimes she thought she'd go mad from the wind. It never seemed to stop. Not even in the summer, according to Rand.

The fire was almost out as they stepped inside Amelia's quarters.

Emmie knelt by the wood stack. "I'll get the fire going." The wind blew down the chimney and sent ashes flying all over her and into the room as she opened the stove door. She quickly threw two logs in and shut the door again.

"Let's just have some of last night's stew since we'll be having tea with Frances," Amelia said. "I'm really not that hungry, are you?"

"Not at all," Emmie said. "That would be lovely. I'll warm it up." She opened the back door and lifted the brick off the pan sitting on the ground. There were too many roving dogs to set the pan out without something heavy on the lid. She put the pan on the stove and turned to tie on an apron.

"I feel sorry for poor Frances," Amelia said.

"Why should you feel sorry for her?" Emmie said. "She seems happy enough."

"Her husband, Lieutenant Grummond, doesn't seem to give her much thought. He's always out playing poker at the sutler's store or trying to stir up some of the men to go on some confrontation with the Indians. Mrs. Horton says this is his second marriage. I have a feeling it won't be long before his hot blood puts him in harm's way. And poor little Frances is so loyal and sweet."

"But aren't most men a lot like that?" Emmie asked as she stirred the stew. "My brothers were and so was Monroe." She turned back around in time to see Sarah and Amelia share a long look.

"Rand and Jake are different, of course," Emmie said hastily. "But you two are luckier than most."

Sarah took her bonnet off and smoothed the fabric of her blue dress. "Actually, Emmie, I'm glad you brought this up. I've wanted to talk to you about your view of men. I've seen the way you shy away from our male callers, even Isaac. I've found most soldiers to be loyal and kind to their wives. And Ben was—Ben was not a good example for you to look to. I hate to see you waste your life because of that distrust you carry around like a shield. I'm sorry to hear Monroe wasn't kind to you."

Emmie flushed. "It's not that he wasn't kind—" She gulped and sat down. She twisted her hands together in her lap as the other women sat beside her. But did she have the strength to tell it? She drew a shaky breath. "I've wanted to tell you about this." She slowly searched the faces of her friends. "But I was afraid you wouldn't care for me anymore when you knew the truth."

Amelia leaned forward and took her hand. "Nothing you say could possibly change how we feel about you, Emmie dear. You're our friend and we love you. Your husband's character can't change yours. You're sweet and loyal and giving. I'm honored to be your friend, and I know Sarah is too. You can tell us anything, and we won't betray your confidence."

Tears welled up in Emmie's eyes. "I–I don't really know how to begin," she choked.

Sarah handed her a hankie. "Begin wherever you want. We have plenty of time."

Emmie twisted the hankie in her hand. "You have to understand. Monroe was so–so *alive* when I met him. I'd never seen anyone with so much exuberance and energy. I couldn't resist that vitality. When he began to pay attention to me, I couldn't believe it. Me. The slutty daughter of the town drunk."

"Oh, Emmie, you were never that!" Sarah's voice was indignant.

"I heard Mrs. Lambert call me that once when

I was thirteen. I've never forgotten it. I'd never even talked to a boy besides my brothers when I heard her say that, but I was so ashamed."

"Back in Wabash when I was a girl, my mother always talked about how sweet you were and what a shame it was you had to grow up with the father you had," Sarah said.

The words melted something cold and frozen in Emmie's heart. "Did she really?"

"Really. She would see you at Pap's store. When we'd get home, she'd tell me I should be more like you and not such a tomboy."

A tear trailed down Emmie's cheek. "She wouldn't say that now. Not if she knew the truth."

"What truth?" Sarah's voice was insistent.

Emmie took another deep breath. "After Monroe's funeral, a lady showed up at my door. Well dressed and pretty with a small boy in her arms. *She* was Monroe's true wife, and the little boy was his son. He'd married me although he was already married to her. That's why I had to leave town."

Sarah's green eyes widened and a horrified understanding crept into her expression. "You mean . . . your marriage to Monroe wasn't real?"

Emmie nodded. "And the baby I'm carrying is a bastard. I'm sure Mrs. Lambert is saying she was right about me all along."

The seconds seemed like hours as the shock registered on the faces of her friends. Where would she go if they threw her out? Maybe she should never have told them.

Amelia jumped to her feet and pulled Emmie into an embrace. "You poor dear."

Sarah took her hand. "It's not your fault, Emmie. You didn't know."

Hot blood rushed to her cheeks and she bowed her head. "That's not what they're saying back in Wabash, I'm sure. I was beginning to get some strange looks before I left."

"But we know you too well to believe any lies," Amelia said. "Why didn't you tell us sooner? Surely you knew we would believe you?"

"I didn't know what to do. It hurt too much to talk about or even think about." She hurried to stir the stew before it burned. She turned around. "I can't tell you how much better it feels now that you know the truth. I've felt badly about deceiving you both. And now you know why I can never trust another man. It hurts too much when you find out all that sweet talk is a lie."

Amelia kissed her cheek. "Emmie, dear, God has someone very special in mind for you. You'll see. But your secret is safe with us. Now let's have some of that stew."

THREE

Isaac tugged his jacket up around his throat and sat back in the saddle. The October wind swept the plains that blended into rolling hills that could hide hostiles.

Rand reined in his horse beside him and squinted at the hills. "See something?"

"No, just looking." Isaac glanced at his friend from the corner of his eye. Emmie was living in his household. Maybe Rand could offer some advice. "Emmie seemed a little standoffish today at church. Is she feeling all right?"

Wariness crept into Rand's brown eyes. "I think so. The courting isn't going so well?"

"One minute she seems to smile my way and the next she's hiding behind Sarah's skirts and rushing off to help Amelia with something."

The wind tried to lift Rand's hat from his head, and he settled it more securely. "I think she had a rough time in her first marriage. She's apt to be a little skittish."

"I can be a patient man."

A grin lifted Rand's good-natured face. "I can't say as I've noticed."

Isaac grinned back. "I'd pray for patience but it might make it worse." He squinted in the sun glinting off the snow but saw nothing move. "I fear it will be years before homesteading is safe here, but I found some land near Sheridan. I think I'm going to buy it. There's a parcel next to the one I have my eye on. You interested?"

Rand's eyes widened. "You bet I am! Adjoining ranches would be better for the women too. Less lonesome."

"You're assuming I'll be successful in my bid for Emmie's hand. I'm not so sure."

Rand picked up the reins and started toward the hills. "Emmie will come around. Give her time."

Isaac stared at his friend's back. Rand knew something he wasn't ready to tell. But at least he knew to give Emmie space. Isaac would back off and see if she showed any distress from it.

The sun shone weakly in a pale-blue sky as Emmie held on to her skirt and hurried across the parade ground with Sarah and Amelia. Frances met them at the door with tears in her eyes and ushered them in out of the cold wind to join her and Mrs. Horton.

"Why, Frances, dear. Whatever is the matter?" Amelia put an arm around the petite young woman, and Frances promptly burst into sobs.

"I was trying to fix some stew for my husband as a surprise. Our cook was late, and I thought I'd try a recipe Mrs. Horton gave me. She said it was foolproof. But she didn't tell me how much of that hateful pressed vegetable cake to put in, so I broke off what I thought was the right amount." She sobbed and pointed to the kitchen. "Now look. And I wanted it to be so perfect for my first tea party," she wailed.

Globs of stew ran over the big pot and lay deposited like a sticky surprise on the floor. The smell of scorched potatoes and carrots burned their noses with an acrid smoke.

Sarah made a strange, strangling noise, and Emmie looked at her in surprise. Was she laughing? She looked closer. Yes, she definitely was, although she was making a valiant attempt to suppress her mirth.

"I'm sorry," Sarah gasped finally, wiping the tears of laughter from her eyes. "I'm just so relieved to find out I'm not the only one who's done something like this. Ask Rand to tell you about my first attempt to cook with those desiccated vegetables."

Frances sobbed one last time, but a glimmer of smile appeared at the corners of her sweetly curving lips. "You did it too?"

"I did indeed. Only I made a much bigger mess. Don't fret. We'll help you clean it up, and then we'll have tea by the fire."

"I just knew we were going to be good friends!" Frances clapped in delight, then showed them to her rags and water.

Mrs. Horton rinsed out her rag, then ran her plump hands over her skirt to dry them. "I hear another lady is joining our little band. Major DuBois is bringing his daughter, Jessica."

"Oh no!" Sarah and Amelia spoke in unison.

"You know her?" Emmie asked.

Amelia colored and lowered her eyes. "I don't like to speak ill of anyone, but Jessica—" She broke off and bit her lip.

Sarah nodded. "Jessica was engaged to Rand when I got out West. And she arranged for Indians to kidnap me to get me away from Rand. I've really tried to get over the way I feel about her, but she makes it hard for any woman to be a real friend to her."

"Oh my!" Mrs. Horton fanned herself. "I shall want to hear the full story someday."

"I'm sure she has her good points," Amelia said. "But Sarah is right—it's hard to find them. But maybe she's changed."

"You always see the good in people," Sarah said with a loving look at her friend. "You can never seem to admit that some people are just plain rotten through and through. Like—" She broke off with an apologetic look at Emmie.

"Like Ben," Emmie finished for her. "You don't have to mince words on my account, Sarah." She glanced at Mrs. Horton. "When is she coming?"

Mrs. Horton fanned her flushed face. "Any day now. Oh dear, this could be a real conundrum. My husband will report to the major, her father. I must be polite to her."

"It's going to be a long winter." Amelia sighed.

The next day was colder and more like they had expected late autumn to be. The wind blew ferociously, and the sky was overcast. Emmie offered to take the laundry to Suds Row. Amelia was feeling poorly and let herself be talked into some hot tea with Sarah while Emmie ran across the parade ground to the laundresses' cabins and tents. As she passed the sutler's store on the way back, she saw a group of men all clustered around, looking in the windows. Curious, she sidled up behind Rooster and tried to see around his scrawny neck.

"Howdy, Miss Emmie." He flushed and backed away from the window a bit.

"What's going on, Rooster?"

"Nothin' much. The men's jest curious about the new gal that come in with the supply train a couple of days ago. She's the daughter of Major DuBois and sure is a looker. Not that it matters to me, of course. She's in there with her pappy and Lieutenant Liddle."

Something squeezed tightly in Emmie's chest. Was Isaac interested in Miss DuBois? She stood on tiptoe and looked in the window. The young woman inside was a real beauty with deep-red curls tied back at her long, slim neck. Her dark-blue gown enhanced her voluptuous figure, and the lace at the neck framed an exquisitely delicate face. She clung to Isaac's arm and gazed up at him adoringly with big blue eyes.

Isaac was smiling down at her indulgently. He turned slightly and saw Emmie looking in the window. His eyes widened as they met hers, and he raised a hand involuntarily.

Jessica turned to see what he was looking at. She clutched his arm tighter and said something that caused the other men to laugh.

Emmie fled back to the safety of the Campbell quarters. She fought the tears prickling at the back of her throat. Jessica really was a beauty. And an aristocratic one. With her father's help, a young officer could go far. Why was she so upset, anyway? Emmie had made it perfectly clear to Isaac that she wasn't interested.

For the next few days, Emmie threw herself into helping Sarah. She didn't want to have any time to think. They spent their afternoons with the other women of the fort, stitching tiny garments for the coming babies and learning about child care from the experienced mothers. They worked on Amelia's layette since her baby was due first. They wanted to make sure everything was ready.

Amelia stitched at the final quilt in her baby's layette. "I wonder where Isaac has been. We haven't seen him in several days."

"I noticed that a couple of days ago and asked Rand about it," Sarah said. "He said he'd invited him over for dinner several times, but Isaac always had an excuse. He's been acting strange, Rand said. Not his usual cheerful self. And Rand said he thought Jessica had set her cap for him now."

Emmie's heart clenched. Wasn't it what she

wanted? At least she wouldn't have to tell Isaac the truth about her so-called marriage.

"Not Isaac!" Amelia's voice was alarmed. "We must do something, Sarah."

"I don't think she'll get 'round him." Sarah bit off the thread and smoothed the block she was sewing, then sighed. "I know we should stop by and call on her. It's been hard to get enough courage."

Emmie kept her gaze on her needlework, but her heart thumped uncomfortably. She wasn't at all sure she wanted to meet this woman.

Amelia stared across the room at Emmie. "Maybe you should invite him over, Emmie. I thought he seemed to be sweet on you. If you were nice to him, maybe we could get him out of Jessica's clutches."

"I've told you before I don't intend to get involved with any man," Emmie said. "It wouldn't be right with my situation."

"But Isaac is different," Sarah said. "He's like Rand and Jake. He has character and principles."

"Then I hope he'll see through Jessica on his own." Emmie's tone did not invite further discussion.

Amelia gave a sidelong glance at Sarah. "We'll just have to trust in his good sense."

The thick paper rustled in Isaac's pocket, and he stood a little straighter as he strode into the sutler's store. The scent of cinnamon blended with that of tallow and kerosene swirled in the air as he shut the heavy door behind him to block out the cold wind. The rows of supplies were barely wide enough to allow his broad shoulders through, but he pressed toward the front of the store. He'd seen Emmie come in a few minutes ago.

She turned away from the candy counter near the front of the store and longingly glanced back toward the licorice.

He motioned to the clerk behind the counter. "A licorice for the lady, please."

The blue cape she wore deepened the color of her violet eyes as she whirled to face him. "I don't need it, Lieutenant Liddle. It's much too dear."

"I'm celebrating today." He handed her the small bag of licorice and smiled. "I'm a landowner."

Her small gloved hand circled the bag, and she peeked inside as if she couldn't wait to taste the candy. "A landowner?"

He pulled the deed from his pocket. "I just bought five hundred acres near Sheridan."

The color washed from her cheeks. "You're leaving the fort?"

The desolation in her face encouraged him. She didn't want him to leave. "Not yet. I've got two years to serve yet, but I want to be ready. By then the area should be safe enough. I'd like to show it to you sometime."

Her long lashes swept down and obscured the expression in her eyes. "What does it look like?"

"It's only five miles away, so it looks a lot like here."

"That seems a little dangerous in more ways than one. The Indian trouble is far from over."

"This territory is perfect for cattle and horses, and I didn't want to miss a good opportunity. Would you come see it with me?"

She bit her lip. "I don't know what the future will bring."

"I'd like a woman's opinion. Promise you'll at least come look at it with me."

She moved the bag of candy to her other hand. "I don't like to make promises I might not be able to keep."

"This one will be easy. We'll take a picnic and some other soldiers as soon as it seems safe. Please?"

"Very well. But only if Rand says it's safe."

She took a step toward the door, and he knew it was too soon to tell her he dreamed of building her a home on those rolling hills. He'd told Rand he could be patient, but it was getting harder than he realized.

FOUR

Hurry up, Sarah. We're going to be late," Emmie called at the bedroom door. "Assembly sounded five minutes ago, and the post band is warming up."

"I'm coming!" Sarah rushed out in a flurry of rustling skirts and the wafting aroma of lilac. Emmie and Joel followed her out the door and across the parade ground toward the milling crowd in front of headquarters. They hurried up the platform that Colonel Carrington had ordered erected for the ladies and found a seat beside Amelia.

"I thought you were going to miss the opening assembly," Amelia whispered.

Lieutenant Adair, adjutant of the Eighteenth, had the adjutant's call sounded. The companies formed lines in front of their quarters, then moved to their battle positions. Colonel Carrington stepped to the fore and addressed the men. He began a stirring address to dedicate the fort to the brave men who had lost their lives in the course of the fifteen weeks it took to erect the encampment.

Emmie found her eyes straying to Isaac's erect figure just to her left near the newly finished flagpole. He kept his eyes steadfastly on his commanding officer, and she felt a thrill of enjoyment that she could look at him without anyone noticing. He looked very fine with his new blue uniform pressed and the sun glinting off his brass epaulets and polished boots. She glanced to her right and saw Jessica DuBois glaring at her. Emmie's cheeks warmed, and she looked away quickly and fastened her gaze on Colonel Carrington.

The little colonel finished his speech by handing the halyards to William Daley, who had done most of the work on the flagpole. The men stood at parade rest with their right hands raised as the orders were barked out. "Attention! Present arms."

The rifles slapped in the hands of the soldiers, and the drum corps played a long roll, followed by the swell of the full band playing "The Star-Spangled Banner." Tears slid down Emmie's cheeks as the guns opened fire, and William Daley pulled the halyards and raised the twenty-by-thirty-six-foot flag slowly to the top of the mast. The chilly breeze stretched it out to its full glory.

She waved her handkerchief in honor of the flag with the rest of the ladies and wept unashamedly. For the first time in her life, she felt part of something worthwhile, something good. She glanced involuntarily over at Isaac and found his steady gaze on her. He smiled and tipped his plumed hat. She smiled tremulously back at him. Glancing over at Jessica, she found her engaged in a conversation with Colonel Carrington. Thank goodness she hadn't seen the exchange.

As the men marched off to their quarters to the tune of "Hail, Columbia," Isaac pushed his way through the melee and caught Emmie's hand. "Will you save me a dance later? I have to take care of a few duties before I can join the party at headquarters."

Heat flooded her cheeks and pleasure curled around her. "I don't think I'll be dancing. Besides, Jessica might be angry."

He frowned. "What's she got to do with us? Her father is my superior. I've just been helping her get settled in. Believe me, I know the kind of woman she is. Once she heard my family owns a large ranch in Texas, her interest kicked up. She doesn't really care anything about me."

Emmie caught back the smile that wanted to spring to her lips. "She doesn't know about the estrangement?"

He shook his head. "It's none of her business. But it's clear you don't think much of me." He strode off in the direction of the barracks.

Emmie bit her lip. Maybe she shouldn't go to the party at all. She just didn't know how to handle Isaac. Or her own turmoil. For just a moment she longed to be free of the mistrust she felt about men. But it was the only defense she had. And she needed a defense when it came to Isaac. There was something about him that so attracted her and made her feel undone.

Amelia grabbed her hand. "Wasn't it wonderful? I was so overcome." She tugged her toward the line of ladies and officers heading toward the door to headquarters. "I don't want to miss a moment of the fun. Sarah went to find Rand and Jake. I told her we'd meet them there."

"I'm not sure I should go. I'm still in mourning—" She broke off at Amelia's incredulous look.

"Don't be ridiculous, Emmie. Whatever do you have to mourn about? That rascal wasn't even your true husband."

"I don't think we've met yet," a soft, feminine voice behind them spoke. "Won't you introduce us, Amelia?"

Emmie turned to stare into Jessica's blue eyes, and her mouth went dry. Did she hear what Amelia had said? But the beautiful face before her gave no clue.

"Hello, Jessica." Amelia's voice sounded falsely gay to Emmie, but Jessica didn't seem to notice. "I heard you were here. Sarah and I had planned to stop in yesterday, but she was not feeling well."

"Oh?" The one word and upraised eyebrow spoke volumes. *Sure you were,* it said. *Just as I lost no time in coming to see you.*

Amelia flushed at her tone. "Um, this is our dear friend, Emmie Croftner."

"Croftner. Where have I heard that name?" Jessica frowned, a gentle ripple in the smooth perfection of her peaches-and-cream complexion. "You're not related to Ben Croftner?"

"I am. I'm his sister."

"Oh my." For a moment Jessica seemed flustered. "Do forgive me. I'm very pleased to meet you." She held out a tiny gloved hand, and Emmie clasped it briefly. "Well, I do hope to get to know you better in the future. Now I must go. I see Daddy motioning to me." She gave Emmie an enigmatic look before strolling over to her father.

"I wonder what she's up to," Sarah said as she hurried over to them. "It looked as though she was actually being nice."

"I really don't know," Amelia admitted. "Maybe she's changed, but she seemed quite sweet."

The furniture had been cleared out of the big meeting room, and long tables piled with food lined the west end of the room. The wooden floor had been polished to a brilliant sheen that was a trifle slick to walk on. The band was already warming up at the makeshift bandstand at the other end of the room under the wide eyes of the post children clustered about them. Emmie noticed that Sarah's brother, Joel, had his harmonica with him. She looked around the room and saw Jake wave to them from the food table.

"Trust that man to find the food." Amelia laughed as they threaded their way through the crowd. "Eating already?" she asked with a smile.

"Wait till you taste this apple pie." Jacob took an enthusiastic bite. "Mrs. Horton certainly has a way with dried apples." With his brown hair and eyes, he looked enough like Rand to be his twin.

Amelia pretended to be miffed. "Well, you can just eat at her table every night then. I won't inflict my poor attempt at culinary arts on you."

He put an arm around her. "Now you know I like your cooking just fine."

"'Just fine,' he says." She punched him gently in the stomach. "When I've been an army wife as long as Mrs. Horton, maybe I'll have a way with dried apples too."

Emmie gave a wistful chuckle. Sarah and Amelia were so lucky. She pushed the memory of Isaac's smiling eyes away.

The band struck up a lively tune behind them, and Jacob took Amelia into his arms. "Time's a-wastin', gal." Amelia laughed as he swung her onto the dance floor.

Rand claimed Sarah a few moments later, and the officers lined up for a dance with Emmie. She was exhausted within fifteen minutes. The men were so exuberant and determined to have a good time. When there was no lady available, they danced with one another. She passed from one set of arms to another until the faces all became a blur.

"I think this is my dance." Isaac cut in on a young lieutenant with a good-natured grin. He spun Emmie away from the disappointed young man. "You look very lovely tonight."

Emmie looked away, heat rising in her cheeks. "It was a very nice ceremony," she said awkwardly.

"Wasn't it?" He drew her closer as the music changed to a slower song and laid his chin on the top of her head. "You are just the right height." His words were soft with a hint of tenderness.

Emmie felt herself relaxing against his chest. She heard the thud of his heart under her ear and smelled the pine scent of his soap. If they could just stay like this forever. She pulled away slightly. That was how Monroe had trapped her before. With his sweet talk and tender arms. She was soiled goods now too. Isaac wouldn't be interested in her if he knew the truth.

"Isaac, I've been looking for you everywhere," a honeyed voice said. "Daddy wants to talk to you." Jessica laid a gloved hand on his arm and gazed up at him with an adorable pout on her lips.

"I'll be along in a moment." He pulled away from her gently. "Let me get Emmie some punch first."

"No, really, I'm fine." Emmie stepped away from him hastily. "You go on along with Jessica. I've promised the next dance to Jacob."

Isaac hesitated, then allowed Jessica to pull him away. Emmie looked after them with her heart aching.

Jacob arrived and held out his arm. "Amelia is determined not to let me sit by her all evening. She says she likes watching us as much as if she could dance to every song herself." He pulled Emmie into a rollicking dance.

She was breathless by the time they finished. Jacob took her elbow and guided her toward the punch table. He took two cups and handed one to her. "I wanted a chance to tell you how much I appreciated the help you've been to Amelia. She was so lonely and blue before you and Sarah came. I haven't caught her crying once since the two of you arrived."

Heat sprang to Emmie's cheeks. "Sarah is the real miracle worker. You've nothing to thank me for." She looked away and took a sip of punch. Sarah had told her it was just strong tea with citric acid in it, but it was really quite good.

"That's not true, you know," he said with a frown. "I've seen the way you hover in the background trying to make sure neither of the girls is doing too much. You have a sweet, unassuming way of encouragement about you that has really helped Amelia. This pregnancy has been hard on her."

"I'm glad if I've been able to help her. There's no one in the world like Amelia. She's so trusting and sees the best in everyone she meets. I wish I could be more like her."

Jacob smiled. "She's too trusting sometimes. But you're right—there's no one like her."

"You love her very much."

He nodded. "She means everything in the world to me. I don't know what I'd do if anything ever happened to her." He looked over to where Amelia sat chatting with Mrs. Horton. "She seems so frail, sometimes it worries me."

Emmie laid a hand on his arm. "She'll be just fine. Dr. Horton is very pleased with her condition. Women have babies all the time, you know."

Jacob squeezed her hand. "You're right, I'm sure. Anyway, thank you for all your help."

"You're very welcome." She watched him stride over to his wife, whose face lit up as she saw him coming. Emmie couldn't suppress the pang of envy that pierced her heart. Love like that would never be for her. She sighed and took the last sip of her punch before being claimed for another dance.

Isaac shuffled and took a gulp of punch as Emmie danced by on the arm of another soldier. How had she gotten under his skin so quickly?

Jessica tugged on his arm. "Isaac, I'm not used to being ignored." Her lips went into a pretty pout.

He managed a smile in spite of his anger with her at being pulled away with a lie. Her father hadn't wanted to see him at all, though the major was watching the two of them even now. He didn't dare show his displeasure. "Sorry, Miss DuBois. Can I get you more punch or a plate of food?"

"I'd settle for some attention. And please, call me Jessica. We're much too close already to stand on such formality." She spoke a little loudly as Emmie danced past again, as though she wanted Emmie to hear the word *close*.

"As you wish."

She touched her fan to his arm in a flirtatious gesture. "I see you watching Emmie Croftner. She won't do much for your career, you know. Not with her background."

"You mean because of her brother? That's not her fault."

The lamplight gleamed on her vivid red hair and her jewelry caught the light. "That's not exactly what I meant. But I suspect you'll find out all her secrets soon. The whole fort will."

He didn't care for the venom in her voice. "What secrets?"

A smile hovered on her full lips. "You'll see."

FIVE

Emmie slipped out of bed and poured cold water from the cracked pitcher into the bowl on the cloth-covered crate that passed as a bed stand. She shivered as she took a piece of flannel and quickly washed herself in the frigid water. She pulled on her blue wool dress and combed her hair up into a serviceable knot, then draped her shawl around her shoulders. She could hear Rand thumping around in the kitchen as he readied for his day. The clear notes of reveille sounded just as she pushed open the curtain from her bedroom and stepped into the small parlor.

Rand looked up as she entered. "Go on back to sleep. I wouldn't let Sarah get up either. I'll grab some grub at mess so you girls don't have to worry about fixing me breakfast."

"I don't mind."

He patted her shoulder as he strode by and seized his coat. "I know you don't, but I have a busy day today, and I might as well get to it. You get some rest." He opened the door and stepped out into the still-dark morning. "I'll see you tonight," he said before closing the door.

Now what was she supposed to do? She was already dressed and too wide awake to go back to sleep. She tiptoed past Joel, a lump under the covers on the parlor cot with just a tuft of blond hair showing, to the bedroom door and peered in at Sarah.

"Rand wouldn't let me get up," Sarah murmured sleepily when she saw her at the door. "I really should, though. I need to take the laundry to Suds Row."

"I'll do it. I'm already dressed and not a bit sleepy. Would you like some breakfast before I go?"

"No, thanks." Sarah yawned and pulled the quilts up higher on her shoulders. "All I want to do is sleep."

"That's fine. You get some rest. I'll stop over and

check on Amelia after I drop off the laundry." Emmie eased the door closed. She was so glad her own morning sickness had lasted such a short time and she felt well enough to continue to be a help to Sarah. She threw some more wood in the fire, put a pot of coffee on to boil, and cut a slice of bread for breakfast. By the time she slathered jam on it and gulped it and two cups of coffee down, the bugle sounded fatigue call. She gathered up the laundry into a basket and stepped outside, as men from various parts of the fort hurried to fall in and find out what their duties would be for the morning.

The sun was just beginning to send pink streaks across the eastern sky as she skirted the parade ground and hurried toward Suds Row. Every fort had a Soapsuds Row, or Suds Row as it was more commonly called. The laundresses were usually either the wives of enlisted men or immigrant women with red, chapped hands and well-developed muscles in their arms and shoulders.

Emmie stopped at the first tent she came to. A kettle of water belched out lye-scented steam, but the laundress was nowhere in sight. She set her burden down and rubbed her back, a bit sore from the evening's festivities.

As she looked around, she saw a pair of blue eyes regarding her seriously from behind the flap of the tent.

"Hello, what's your name?"

The child didn't answer but cautiously stepped out from the protecting flap. A small girl about two years old with a tangled mass of nearly black curls, big blue eyes, and chubby dimpled cheeks gazed up at her.

"Aren't you adorable! Won't you tell me your name?"

The little girl popped a thumb in her mouth, then took it out long enough to say "Mary," before sticking it back in her mouth.

"Well, Mary, do you know where I might find your mama?" Emmie knelt in front of the tiny girl and touched the dark curls.

At that moment a young woman scurried from behind the tent with an armload of uniforms. "Sorry I am if ye had to wait, missy," she gasped in a broad Irish lilt. "I didn't know ye were here." Her face softened as she saw Emmie kneeling before the little girl. "I be seeing you've made the acquaintance of me sister."

Sister? Emmie had assumed the child was the woman's daughter. They both possessed the same dark curls and deep blue eyes. But as she looked closer, she realized the young woman was hardly more than a child herself. Certainly no more than fifteen or six-teen. "Are you the laundress, or should I talk to your mother?" she asked hesitantly.

The young woman dropped the uniforms beside the kettle of water. "Sure and it's myself, Maggie O'Donnell, you'll be wanting, miss. Me mam, God rest her soul, has been with the angels these last two years. The childbed fever took her when Mary here was only six days old."

"I'm sorry." Emmie was intrigued with the energetic young woman. A child raising a child. Judging from her accent, she wasn't too long out of the potato fields of Ireland. "How long have you been in America?"

Maggie dumped a uniform into a galvanized tub and proceeded to scrub it vigorously against the wash-board. "Me da brought us to the wondrous city of New York just four months before Mary arrived. He took a job with the railroad and moved us to Chicago. But the Lord saw fit to take him of the consumption before he clapped eyes on Mary." She leaned forward and said in a whisper, "Between you and me, miss, I think me mum died of a broken heart. She had no reason to go on with me da gone."

"And you've been all alone since?"

"Just me and Mary taking care of each other."

"How did you get out here in the wilderness?" Emmie was fascinated by the young woman's self-confidence and independence.

"A chum of me da's heard the army had a need for a washerwoman out here and arranged for me to have the job. It's hard work, it is, but honest." She saw the expression on Emmie's face. "But don't feel sorry for me, miss. It's better work than I could get in Chicago. The only offer I had there was in a bawdy house. But I'd have taken even that if it meant the difference between watching young Mary starve or no." Maggie stood and pushed a stray black curl out of her eyes. "When you be needing your laundry done by?"

"Tomorrow is soon enough." The last thing Emmie wanted to do was add to this young woman's burden.

"Won't be no problem at all. It's been real nice talking to you. Most ladies don't bother with the likes of me." Maggie grinned cheerfully. "Not that I'm complaining, mind you. I don't have nothing in common with those highfalutin' types anyhow. But you're different, miss."

"Please call me Emmie." She held out her hand.

Maggie eyed her outstretched hand cautiously

before wiping her own water-roughened hand against her apron and taking Emmie's fingers gingerly. "Pleased to meet you, Miss Emmie."

"Just Emmie. I'd like to be friends." She didn't know why it was so important to her, but it was. Something about the young woman drew her irresistibly. She didn't know if it was Maggie's indomitable spirit or harsh circumstances, but Emmie just knew that she wanted to be able to call her a friend.

Maggie's eyes grew wide. "Friends with the likes of me?" Unexpectedly, her eyes welled with tears. "Don't mind me," she sniffled. "Ever since we got here, it's like I'm a spirit or something. The other ladies all look through me, and I can tell they think Mary is me own lovely daughter and that I'm an indecent woman."

Emmie's throat grew thick with her own tears. What would everyone think of her if they knew the truth? "I'll be back tomorrow."

Emmie waved to little Mary and set off toward Amelia's quarters. She was awed by Maggie's spirit and courage. At least Emmie had Sarah and Rand to look to for support. The young washerwoman had no one but was still able to smile at circumstances and find a way to support herself and her sister with honest hard work. Was she a Christian, too, like the Campbells? Maggie's courage shamed her.

Emmie rapped once on Amelia's door and slipped inside. The curtains hadn't been opened yet, though it was afternoon. "Amelia? Are you all right?"

Amelia looked up with a forced smile from her seat on the cot that served as a sofa in the parlor. "I was hoping you'd stop by. I was just sitting here feeling sorry for myself." Her smile was gone and tears hung on her dark lashes.

"Why, whatever is wrong?" Emmie quickly crossed the room to put her arms around her.

"I'm just being a silly goose." Amelia sniffed. "For the first time I'm really frightened about having this baby. What if something's wrong with it? Or I could die and leave Jake all alone with a child to raise. Women do die in childbirth, you know."

Emmie hugged her. "You'll be fine, I know. You're strong and healthy," she said with more conviction than she felt. She and Sarah had discussed how fragile their friend had been looking the last few weeks.

"I'm not afraid to die. I know I'll be with the Lord, but I just don't want to leave Jacob all alone." Amelia scrubbed at her cheeks with the back of her hand, then turned and looked Emmie squarely in the face. "There is one thing you could do that would make me feel better."

"Anything. You want a cup of tea?" Emmie half rose to her feet, but Amelia pulled her back down and gripped her arms.

"I want you to promise that if anything happens to me, you'll marry Jacob and take care of him and the baby."

Emmie caught her breath. What was Amelia saying? She tried to draw away, but Amelia kept a tight grip on her arms.

"I mean it, Emmie. I've thought about it a lot. It would solve your problems too. Jacob would love your baby. He loves children, you know. It would make me feel so much better if I was sure they would be all right no matter what happens."

Emmie couldn't think with Amelia's beseeching blue eyes fastened on her. How could she ask such a thing? But Amelia had never been like other women. She always thought of others first and never seemed to consider her own feelings.

"You can't just plan Jacob's life for him like that," she said desperately.

"He has already agreed. He pooh-poohed my fears, but he said he'd do whatever I wanted if the worst happened."

For an instant, an image of Isaac's auburn hair and blue eyes swam across Emmie's vision, but she pushed it away. That wasn't reality. Her friend was reality. But really, what were the odds of anything happening to Amelia? She was just suffering from pregnancy jitters. Everything would be fine. She just needed a little assurance right now.

"I promise," she said.

Amelia smiled. "I feel so much better. Now I'll take that cup of tea."

SIX

Such a lovely day with winter right around the corner. The buglers sounded a tune as Emmie hurried along the path to her house. She couldn't wait to tell Sarah about Maggie. The cabin smelled of pine sap, wood smoke, and rising bread dough when Emmie slipped inside and found Sarah in the kitchen kneading dough.

Emmie hung her cloak on the hook by the door and went to wash her hands. "I must tell you about the laundress I met." She launched into a description of Maggie.

Sarah gave the dough a pat and set it aside. "I think

it's lovely for you to befriend her, and we can certainly have her to tea. But you should know that the other women will disapprove. Army life is so regulated, and fraternizing with the enlisted men is frowned on here."

Emmie put on her apron and took a pan of dough to punch down. "But she's not an enlisted man. She's just a lonely young woman with no friends. I don't see how being a friend to her could hurt."

"I know it's hard to understand. But there's a very rigid code of behavior in the army, and the laundresses are considered beyond polite society by most gentlewomen."

Emmie stared at her in bewilderment. "The one thing I've always noticed about army people is how friendly they are and how easily they welcome new people to the post. Why would they feel that way about someone who earns her living by her own hard work?"

"It really goes back to when laundresses were kept women who followed after the troops to see to the needs of their men. In the past, many were—well I don't like to say it—but they were scarlet women. Nowadays, many are wives of enlisted men too. Fraternizing with an enlisted man's wife is just the same as being friends with him."

"What does that say about someone like me?"

"I'm sorry if I upset you, Emmie. I just wanted you to know what the situation is like here. I would love to meet young Maggie."

"You're skirting my question. What if Jessica overheard us talking? If people knew about Monroe, my reputation would be much worse than Maggie's. Maybe I should leave. If your other friends would frown on associating with Maggie, they would be disgusted with me too. The truth will come out sooner or later. It always does."

Sarah rubbed her floury hands on her apron, then touched Emmie's arm. "Anyone who knows you at all knows you're trusting and innocent. You were deceived by a scoundrel. No one would blame you. You put any thought of leaving us right out of your head. Besides, it's much too dangerous right now to even think about leaving the fort."

Emmie looked out the window at the blue hills around the fort. The shame she'd pushed to the back of her mind swelled up again. No amount of love and acceptance would erase it. Maybe she should just confess it to the world instead of trying to pretend to be something she wasn't. She was sure Jessica wouldn't be as charitable about her innocence as Amelia and Sarah had been.

As November began, winter settled its icy claws more firmly into the little fort community. Piercing winds, mountains of snowdrifts, and bitter cold kept the ladies constantly looking for ways to keep warm. The wood details, escorted by guards, went out every day but could barely keep up with the demand, even though wood had been stockpiled for several months. The ladies ventured out only when absolutely necessary. Even a brisk walk from quarters to quarters left them numb with cold.

Emmie couldn't remember a time when she didn't ache with cold. The wind howled around the tiny fort like a pack of ravenous wild dogs, poking icy fangs through her skirts that chilled her to the bone.

The sun had barely come up when she bundled her cloak around her as tightly as she could before picking up her basket and heading for the sutler's store. Sarah had been craving fruit, any fruit, so Emmie thought she would see what was available. The price would be dear, but Rand had told her to get whatever she could find. He worried a lot about his wife these days. Sarah seemed pale and listless, but Emmie thought it was the confinement of the tiny fort and the especially cold weather they'd been enduring that caused her friend's wan appearance.

There had been constant skirmishes with the Indians, and the little graveyard beside the fort received a newly fallen soldier almost every day. The ever-present fear hung like black crepe over the encampment.

She staggered to keep her balance in the wind as she hurried as fast as she could toward the sutler's store. As she passed the DuBois residence, she saw Jessica. Though Emmie would have hurried by without a greeting, Jessica motioned to her, bidding her to come to the door. What now? She stopped for a moment before obeying her imperious summons. She had managed to avoid any contact with Jessica since the dance.

The cold air followed her into the foyer as Jessica shut the door behind them. Emmie glanced around as she followed Jessica into the parlor. The fireplace blazed with warmth and cast a golden glow over the gleaming mahogany furniture. The parlor looked lovely and welcoming, but the look on Jessica's face was just the opposite.

"I've been watching for you," Jessica said. "You haven't been out much." Her eyes swept contemptuously over Emmie's plain gray dress and bonnet.

"Sarah hasn't been well. I really can't stay. I need to get back to her as quickly as possible." Emmie shrank away from the brittle smile on Jessica's face. She couldn't imagine what Jessica would want with her. And what did that triumphant glint in her eye mean? Emmie's nervousness increased a notch as Jessica allowed a strained pause to drag out.

"This won't take long," she said finally with another chilly smile. "I just thought it was important that we get a few things settled between us."

"What kinds of things?" Emmie's agitation grew as Jessica stepped in closer. Her sweet, overpowering scent made Emmie's head swim.

"I've seen the way you look at Isaac. My father wants me to marry him, and I intend to do just that. Rand chose Sarah, that chit of a girl, over me for reasons I cannot fathom. I want you to know that I refuse to be humiliated again." She pushed her face into Emmie's. "I know all about you, Miss Croftner.

After I overheard a comment you made, I contacted a cousin who made some inquiries for me. I know that the child you're carrying is a bastard and you've never been married. If you force me to, I'll let everyone here know all about it."

Emmie felt faint. This was her nightmare come true. She couldn't stand for anyone to know about her shame. It would reflect on her friends too. She clutched icy hands in the folds of her cloak and swallowed hard.

Jessica smiled again. "You are to stay away from Isaac. Make it clear you have no interest in him at all. If you don't, I'll let everyone know you lived with a man out of wedlock."

"But I thought I was married! It wasn't like you're making it sound."

"If you were too stupid to figure out what the man was after, that's your problem." Jessica flicked a disparaging hand at Emmie. "Oh, you're not unattractive, I suppose. That helpless look probably brings out the protective nature in some men. But you're no better than your brothers, and anyone who knew them would instantly know what kind of person you are behind that little-girl-lost facade."

Emmie struggled to catch her breath. Jessica was

only saying the things Emmie felt inside. She stiffened her shoulders. "You needn't worry about me, Miss DuBois. I have no interest in Isaac. He is merely a friend."

Jessica's eyes narrowed as she stared at Emmie. "I certainly hope that's true. For your sake, it had better be." She opened the door and practically pushed Emmie through it. "And don't tell anyone about our conversation. Not if you want your little secret to remain between the two of us."

Emmie found herself staring at the brass knocker as the door slammed behind her. She gulped and forced herself to walk down the steps on shaky legs.

The walk in the cold wind stiffened Emmie's resolve, and she had quit shaking by the time she pushed open the door to the sutler's store. The smell struck her as she stepped across the threshold. The overpowering stench of unwashed bodies mixed with cinnamon, coffee, tobacco, and vinegar from the pickle keg nearly gagged her. She quickly picked up a handful of wrinkled apples and paid for them, aware of the stares of the Indians and soldiers alike. The sutler's store was always such a trial to endure. It wasn't so bad when she was escorted by Rand or Jake, but a young woman alone attracted a lot of attention.

She escaped into the fresh air and hurried back to the Campbell quarters. Sarah looked up as she burst through the door. Emmie had intended to tell her friend about the confrontation with Jessica, but after one look at Sarah's pale, pinched face, she decided against it. Now was the perfect time to put into practice what she'd been learning the past few weeks. She would turn the whole matter over to God. She put on a bright smile as she closed the door behind her.

She pulled out an apple and showed it to Sarah. "I found some lovely apples at the sutler's store. They're a little wrinkly, but they don't seem to have any bad spots. Here, smell." She put a small apple under Sarah's nose. "They should make delicious apple dumplings."

Sarah took the apple slowly and sniffed. A ghost of a smile brightened her face, then she lay back against the cushions on the parlor cot. "You are a dear." She handed the apple back to Emmie. "I don't know why I feel so poorly. The winter is just beginning and already the wind is about to drive me mad."

Emmie sat beside her and put an arm around her slim shoulders. "God is here with you, though. I have so much peace since I realized that. Now the vastness that used to terrify me when I looked around outside just reminds me how powerful he is."

Sarah smiled at her. "You put me to shame sometimes, Emmie. You're right, of course. At least I'm here with Rand and not stuck back East with my brother. With all the fighting going on, Rand hasn't been seriously wounded and neither has Jacob. We should count our blessings."

Emmie hugged her again. "I think I'll get started on those apple dumplings. You rest a while." She stood and went to the kitchen, all of three steps away. She hummed as she took down her apron and wrapped it around her waist. Hmm, it seemed her waist had thickened just since yesterday. She took down a tin of flour and dumped some into a bowl. "What time did Rand say to expect him?"

"He sent Joel by to tell us he'd be late. That reckless Lieutenant Fetterman has finally talked Colonel Carrington into letting him try an ambush. The colonel asked Rand to go along to keep Fetterman out of trouble. They're taking some mules as bait, but Joel said Rand thought it was a harebrained scheme. Red Cloud is no fool, but Fetterman is hotheaded and thinks all Indians are stupid and slow."

Emmie sighed. Always there was fighting. Every day, every hour, they listened for the crack of rifles in the winter air and the war whoops of the Sioux. There was never a respite. As she mixed the dough and sliced the apples, she and Sarah chatted about everything except the one thing they both listened for. Through the long afternoon and early evening, they waited and talked to fill the time. Only when they heard Rand's boot heels and Joel's excited chatter as they came up the front porch did they relax.

Rand came in, stomping his feet in the entry and reminding Joel to do the same. His face was pale and pinched with the cold. Sarah rushed to help him out of his snow-covered greatcoat. He shrugged it off and dropped onto the cot with a sigh. He held out his hands toward the roaring fire as Sarah sat beside him.

"I expected you before now," she said softly.

"You should have seen it," Joel put in excitedly. "I was watching from the blockhouse. The Sioux knew it was a trap. They just waited Fetterman out, then slipped behind the fort and stampeded the cattle. Fetterman looked as savage as a meat ax."

"Joel!" Sarah spoke sharply.

He looked sheepish. "Well, that's what Rooster said."

"You're not to talk disrespectfully of your elders."

Her brother scuffed a toe on the floor. "He sure was mad, though. He told the colonel he wanted to go out after them right then and there, but the colonel wouldn't let him. He stomped off with Lieutenant Grummond. They were both grumbling."

Emmie broke in hurriedly. "Your supper's ready." She didn't want to hear about any more battles. She watched as Sarah put a hand on Rand's arm, then hurried to fix him a plate of thick stew and warm slices of bread with butter. She fixed a smaller plate for Joel.

"Joel's right," Rand said after a few bites of supper. "Fetterman is spoiling for a fight with the Sioux. He's going to wind up with his hair lifted if he isn't careful. He's rash, and I'm afraid he'll drag Lieutenant Grummond into a losing battle with him. Neither one of them have any respect for the way an Indian can fight. They haven't been out here long enough to have a little sense knocked into them."

Emmie shuddered. She'd seen Lieutenant Fetterman around. He usually had a group of starry-eyed soldiers around listening to stories of his exploits in the War Between the States. His bragging and posturing repelled her and filled her with a strange foreboding.

SEVEN

Isaac stamped his cold feet outside the Campbell house and hit his fist on the door. His greatcoat did little to stop the icy wind from chilling him through and through.

The door opened, and he looked down into Emmie's face. Her eyes widened when she saw him. Was that a flicker of fear in her eyes? Why would she ever be fearful of him?

The snow swirled around him like a thick, wet fog

that skated onto the kitchen floor. She stepped out of the way. "Come in."

He pushed past her and she shut the door. He looked around the kitchen and fastened his gaze on Sarah sitting at the table. "We've got a visitor. I told her to come in with me, but she insisted I come and ask permission."

Sarah looked up at him anxiously. "Is Amelia all right?"

Isaac grinned, imagining her response once she knew. "It's got nothing to do with her. This is a visitor the Lord has blown our way. I think you'll be right happy to see her."

Sarah gave him a fierce look, and he laughed. "I think it should be a surprise in spite of what she says." He turned and opened the door again. "Come on in."

A figure covered in a thick buffalo hide slowly stepped through the doorway. His chest squeezed now that he could see her in better light. Snow coated her thick black braids, and she looked pale and emaciated.

Morning Song had been one of Sarah's Sioux students at Fort Laramie until she left with her band to join Red Cloud. Most of them had thought they'd never see her again, especially after Ben Croftner mistreated her.

Morning Song stared straight at Sarah, then smiled. "My Sarah, do you not know me?"

Sarah gasped and jumped to her feet. "Morning Song!" She ran toward the young woman with her arms outstretched. "I didn't know if I'd ever see you again." She put her arms around the young woman and hugged her.

Morning Song returned the hug, then stepped back. She shrugged off the buffalo robe and revealed a baby snuggled against her breast in an Indian carrier of some sort. The child, a boy, slept peacefully with his thumb corked in his mouth.

"Oh, Morning Song, you have a baby!" Sarah held out her hands. "May I?"

The Indian girl nodded and gently lifted her child out of the carrier and put him into Sarah's outstretched arms. Sarah cradled him and crooned to him. Isaac stared too. The baby was obviously Ben's.

Morning Song had once been so beautiful. Now her hair was dull and lifeless from hunger and deprivation, and the sparkle was gone from her large dark eyes.

Joel jumped up from the table. "Morning Song, is Red Hawk with you? Can I see him?"

Morning Song's face sobered and she shook her

head. "I come alone, little warrior." She touched Joel's shoulder.

Isaac noticed Emmie standing off with her hands clenched together. This would affect her, too, though she didn't know it yet. He moved over to stand beside her so he could speak without being overheard. "Morning Song was one of Sarah's first students back at Fort Laramie when she taught reading and writing to the Indian youngsters."

How did he explain such a delicate situation? He glanced at Morning Song and Sarah. They were talking so they wouldn't hear this. "Um, your brother Ben was, uh, married. Well, not really married." He broke off in embarrassment, then plunged ahead. "Anyway, Emmie, that baby is your nephew. Ben had mistreated her, and Sarah got her away from him. She disappeared shortly after that and we haven't seen her since. She came in a little while ago with some friendly Shoshone."

Emmie looked across the room at the sleeping child. "My nephew, Ben's child? Did he know?"

"I don't think so."

"Does she know who I am?"

"I didn't tell her. To tell you the truth, I'd almost

forgotten Ben was your brother. You're very different. You want to meet her?"

Her gaze lingered on Sarah holding the baby, and he saw hunger in Emmie's face. She probably felt as though she had no family.

She nodded. "Could I?"

He touched her arm and guided her closer. This was the nearest he'd been to the baby himself. The little one did have a certain look of her brother. His eyes were the same smoky gray. His hair was darker than Ben's blond hair but not the raven of Morning Song's.

Sarah looked up and saw her standing there. Dawning comprehension filled her face. After a glance at her Indian friend, she gently placed the child into Emmie's arms. "What is his name, Morning Song?"

"I call him John. I learned about John in the Holy Book when I went to the mission school. About how he taught others to love God. So I named him John Randall. My people, my father, they call him Gray Buffalo."

Rand jerked his head up, then a delighted grin stole over his face. "You named him after me?"

Morning Song nodded. "You and Sarah are my friends. I want for John to be a fine man like you. Not like—" She broke off and took a deep breath.

Isaac heard Emmie's intake of breath, and he wished he could embrace her. Her brother was despicable.

Emmie cradled the baby, then took a step closer to Morning Song. "I am your sister. Ben was my brother."

Morning Song flinched back as though Emmie had struck her. She stared at Isaac. "You have her here? Sister of my enemy?"

She whirled as though to flee before she remembered Emmie still held her child. She snatched her son from Emmie's arms, then realized Emmie was crying. She searched Emmie's eyes as if probing secrets from her soul.

The tension eased out of her shoulders, and she gently handed young John back to Emmie. "You are my sister. Ben hurt you too."

Her eyes wide, Emmie accepted the child again. The baby had awakened from all the fuss and played with strands of her dark hair that had escaped their confinement. She hugged him gently, then gave him back to Morning Song. "You have a beautiful son."

Morning Song smiled and murmured to the baby as she eased him back into the carrier. "Ben is here?"

Sarah shook her head. "Oh no, Morning Song. He's—" She broke off and glanced at Emmie.

Emmie finished Sarah's sentence for her. "He's dead. Killed in an attack by Sioux."

Morning Song's forehead wrinkled. "When did this happen?"

"Shortly after you left Fort Laramie. He was killed in a fall from a horse, Labe said."

Morning Song shook her head. "Then it is not Ben. My brother, Red Hawk, saw him near the mountain where the white men took the yellow rock not many moons ago."

Rand glanced at Isaac, then back at Morning Song. "You mean the gold mines in Montana?"

Morning Song nodded. "My brother wanted to kill him, but too many white men were around with guns."

Isaac inhaled and his gaze went to Emmie standing rigidly by the fire. Her violet eyes were wide, and she put her hand to her chest. Her mouth trembled. Was she happy Ben was alive or distressed?

The only sound was the crackle from the fire. Emmie cleared her throat. "But he left Labe behind. Why would he do that?"

Morning Song shrugged. "I do not know. Perhaps

he felt Labe was never fully with him and his schemes. I know your brother Labe felt sorry for the way Ben treated me."

"I can't believe it," Rand said finally. "All this time we were sure he was dead. Do you know if Labe found him in the goldfields?"

"I not know. Red Hawk only saw Ben."

Sarah put her arm around Morning Song. "There's so much to tell you. Come over by the fire and rest. You'll stay here with us, of course."

Morning Song wilted and she gasped. "It is more than I hoped for. I just wished to see you again. I will go back to the camp."

"You'll do no such thing," Rand put in firmly. "You need to rest and get your strength back. We can make up a bed for you in the kitchen near the stove."

"She can have my place here in the parlor," Joel said. "I can stay with Jacob and Amelia."

"Good idea," Sarah said. "Is Red Hawk with you, Morning Song? He can stay with Joel."

The young woman bowed her head. "He and my father are with Red Cloud. I could not stay when I knew they would soon fight against my friends."

Isaac's gut tightened. Red Cloud was preparing for war, massing tribes from all over the Sioux nation. The confrontation was coming soon. Isaac wasn't sure how many of them would survive it.

EIGHT

The dawn brought a blizzard with it as snow joined the howling wind of the night before. The swirling snow blotted out the sun and blew through the cracks in the house. Emmie shivered as she lit her lamp and quickly washed with her flannel and dressed in the blue wool. As she pulled her curtain back, she could hear Morning Song crooning to baby John. She was eager to see both Morning Song and the baby again.

Morning Song looked up from her seat by the

kitchen stove as Emmie hurried toward her. "You are up early. Sarah still sleeping."

Emmie poured hot water into the teapot. "Has Rand left?"

Morning Song nodded as she went to lay the baby down on the mat. She covered him with the edge of the buffalo robe and rejoined Emmie. "He was up most the night. Not used to warm house."

Emmie tried to imagine living out on the plains in a tepee and shivered. She poured herself and Morning Song a cup of tea.

Morning Song smiled as she spooned sugar into her tea and picked up her cup gently. "It has been many moons since I had tea." She sighed and took a sip. "Many changes have come."

Emmie clasped her hands together. "I–I want to tell you how sorry I am about what Ben did to you. He was always . . . difficult. A–And I know about betrayal and how it hurts."

Morning Song nodded. "I see this in your face. You are not your brother. We will be friends."

Sarah opened the bedroom door and stepped into the room. Her eyes were sparkling with excitement. "I had to get up and make sure last night wasn't a dream.

Rand and I talked about it after we went to bed, and we want you and John to stay with us, Morning Song. You can't go back to the Sioux. They didn't treat the baby or you very well. We love you and want you to become part of our family."

Morning Song swallowed hard as she fought tears. Her chin sank to her chest. "I do not wish to be burden for my friends. The Shoshone chief says I can stay at his encampment. But I wish to leave my son with you. My baby deserves to be accepted by whites."

Sarah nodded vigorously. "But we won't keep him without you. You must stay also. Rand has already gone to ask the commander for permission. He's sure the commander will allow it. He is a very compassionate man."

Morning Song lost her battle against the tears and they slid down her cheeks. "I must help you if I stay. John is very good baby. We will try not to disturb my friends."

Sarah smiled. "There will be plenty of crying in a few months anyway. My baby will be born in two months, and Emmie's baby should arrive in May."

Morning Song looked at Emmie. "You do not stay in this house all the time? You have husband here?"

Emmie shook her head slowly. "No husband. Like you, I was not really married, although I thought I was. I am staying here with my friends, just like you."

A ghost of a smile flitted across Morning Song's face. "Rand will act like he eat locoweed after all the babies come."

Three crying babies all close to the same age. The thought made Emmie chuckle. They'd all *want* to eat locoweed.

The snow had finally stopped, so the women donned warm cloaks and bonnets, bundled the baby up, and hurried across the parade ground to show Amelia Morning Song's son. The house was dark when they let themselves in. The fire was almost out.

Emmie went to throw more logs on it. "Sarah, maybe you'd better check on Amelia."

Sarah nodded and hurried to the bedroom. "Amelia?" She turned in the doorway and motioned to Emmie. "The baby's coming!"

Emmie's pulse kicked. She rushed to the bedroom with Morning Song close behind her. A slick sheen of sweat coated Amelia's face and she moaned softly. She was so pale, and Emmie felt a stab of pure terror.

She stepped to the bed and took Amelia's hand. "Your baby will be here soon. You're going to be a mama today."

"Jacob went for Dr. Horton." Amelia moaned again and clung tightly to Emmie's hand. Her eyes opened, and she stared into Emmie's face. "Remember your promise."

Emmie touched her brow, burning hot. "I won't have to remember it. You're going to be fine." But a coldness settled in her belly at the look of Amelia's skin.

Her friend's eyes closed, and she released Emmie's hand. Emmie looked at Sarah's pale face and knew she was in no shape to take charge. "Morning Song, would you go find me some rags and boil some water? And find someone to fetch Jacob. Her labor must have come on suddenly after he left."

The door banged and Jacob rushed in with Dr. Horton close behind. "Thank the Lord you're here. I didn't want to leave her alone, but I had to get the doctor. I kept hoping someone would stop by, but no one was out with the weather so nasty."

They all stepped out of the room so the doctor

could examine her in private. Jacob paced back and forth across the kitchen, pausing now and then to gaze toward the bedroom door. Beyond an initial look of recognition when he saw Morning Song, he withdrew into himself and said nothing to any of them.

Emmie finally took his arm. "Let's pray."

He gave her a startled look. "You're right," he groaned as he dropped to his knees beside a kitchen chair.

Emmie knelt on one side and Sarah and Morning Song on the other. They stayed on their knees for a few more moments, then rose as Dr. Horton came into the room.

"She's in a bad way. She's too weak to stand much of this and the baby is coming the wrong way. Have any of you ladies helped deliver babies before?"

Sarah and Emmie looked at each other and shook their heads.

Morning Song nodded. "I help many women in my village."

Dr. Horton looked at her for a moment, then evidently satisfied with what he saw, nodded. "Wash your hands and come with me. You too," he said to Emmie.

Morning Song and Emmie hurried to obey. They

scrubbed their hands with lye soap and went into the bedroom.

"We've got to try to turn the baby," the doctor said. "Emmie, I need you to hold her down while I push on her stomach. Do you know what to do?" he asked Morning Song.

She nodded and knelt by Amelia. Emmie thought she couldn't stand it as Amelia thrashed and cried out while Morning Song bravely began to turn the baby as gently as she could. Emmie was trembling and dripping with perspiration by the time the doctor stood.

"You can let her go now," he said. "Things should move along now. You did very well," he told Morning Song. "Now both of you get out of here and try to calm Jacob down."

Emmie closed the door behind her with a sense of relief. For a while there, she'd thought they'd lose both Amelia and the baby.

Jacob was beside her instantly. "How is she?" he demanded in a shaky voice.

"We got the baby turned. The doctor says it should be all right now." Emmie washed her hands at the bucket, then went to the stove on shaky legs and poured a cup of coffee.

Amelia cried out behind the closed door and Jacob shuddered convulsively. He sank to a chair and buried his face in his hands. "I can't stand it," he muttered.

The entry door opened and Rand rushed in. "I heard the baby is coming." He stared at Sarah who was crying. He went to embrace her. "She's going to be all right, isn't she?"

Sarah leaned against him and buried her face in his chest. "The doctor thinks so now. But she's very weak."

The afternoon dragged on as they paced outside the bedroom door. Finally Amelia cried out again, then they heard the weak, wavering cry of a newborn baby. Jacob shot to his feet and looked at the bedroom door wildly.

Rand stepped forward and gripped his arm. "Calm down, little brother. You won't do Amelia any good in this state."

Just then the door opened and Dr. Horton stepped through. He looked into Jacob's agonized eyes and smiled reassuringly. "You have a beautiful daughter, Jacob."

Jacob's face was white. "How's my wife?"

The doctor gestured toward the bedroom. "See for yourself."

Jake jumped forward like he was shot out of a cannon. The rest of the family followed him eagerly. Amelia lay against the pillows with a little more color in her cheeks. A tiny face with a tuft of dark hair peeked out from under her arm. Jacob sank to his knees beside his wife and daughter and stared at them with awe on his face.

Amelia smiled up at them. "Isn't she beautiful? I'm glad we decided to name her Gabrielle. 'God's messenger.' She really is a wonderful message from God."

"You're beautiful." Jacob kissed her gently on the forehead, then turned his attention to his daughter. His big hand took her tiny fingers. "She looks just like you."

Amelia smiled. "Does she really?"

"Without a doubt," Rand said.

Sarah stepped closer to the bed. "Aren't you going to hold her, Jacob? First you, then it's my turn."

Amelia lifted the baby and Jacob took her awkwardly. His Adam's apple bobbed as he stared down at his tiny daughter. After a few moments of mutual inspection, he handed the baby to Sarah.

She took her eagerly and snuggled her expertly. "Oh, Amelia, she's adorable!"

Amelia smiled and her eyes closed wearily. Emmie saw her friend's exhaustion and motioned them all out. She was just about to shut the door when Amelia opened her eyes and motioned to her to come back.

"What is it, Amelia?" she said gently. "You need to get some rest."

Amelia clutched her hand. "Thank you. And thank Morning Song for me. You both saved my life. I was so surprised to see her. Tell her I want to have a long talk when I'm stronger."

Emmie smiled and smoothed Amelia's dark hair away from her forehead. "I'll tell her. I told you there was nothing to worry about. You're going to be here to take care of your own husband and baby."

Amelia smiled, then her eyes closed again and Emmie tiptoed out.

NINE

Snow skittered across the walk. Isaac hovered outside the door. It wasn't his place to go inside, but the entire fort had heard Amelia was in grave danger. His feet were lumps of ice, but he couldn't go anywhere until he knew things were okay inside. The doctor had given him some information, but he wanted to make sure.

The door opened and Emmie, swathed in her cloak, stepped through the door. He caught a glimpse of Sarah and Rand sitting on the sofa with contented expressions. Relief loosened the tightness in his chest.

She froze when she saw him, then shut the door behind her. "Isaac, you startled me. Have you been out here long?"

"About an hour." He offered her his arm, and after a brief hesitation, she took it. "Amelia and the baby okay?" He led her across the path toward the Campbell house.

"Yes, thank God. I thought we'd lose her."

He pressed his right hand against her hand resting on his left arm. "I heard you and Morning Song were the heroines of the hour. You're a gritty little thing."

Her steps faltered as reveille sounded. "I didn't do anything but hold her down. Morning Song and the doctor did it all."

"Doc Horton said he had you help because he knew you wouldn't faint. He was pretty sure Sarah would. He said you have a lot of backbone."

"I didn't think I could stand it, but I had to help her. It was awful." Her voice trembled.

Isaac stopped as emotion swirled inside his chest. This feeling that gripped him all the time was more than attraction. He loved this brave little slip of a woman. His fingers tightened over her hand. They belonged together. He wanted to be there when her baby came. No one else could care for her and love her like he could.

He gripped her shoulders and turned her to face him. Her violet eyes looked at him with such trust, and her expression emboldened him. "You've gotten a lot more confident in the past few weeks." He grasped her chin and tilted her head up until he could look into her eyes. "I love you, Emmie. You're all I think about."

She went still, then her lashes shuttered her eyes. "You can't possibly love me, Isaac. Not if you knew . . ."

"Nothing you could tell me would change how I feel." He felt her resistance in the stiff stance of her shoulders and the tilt of her head. "Look at me."

She bit her lip, then her long lashes swept up and emotion blazed in her eyes as he stared into her face. "I'm looking."

"Can you look me in the eye and tell me you don't love me?"

"I–I don't know. I don't want to love you. Love can hurt, Isaac. You don't know what I've been through."

He drew her into the shelter of his arms and rested his chin on her head. "I won't hurt you, my love. From the first moment I laid eyes on you, I knew you were the one I'd been waiting for. I want to be your baby's father. I've seen the gentle, loving spirit you have. You may not want to love me, but I think you do." He drew back and tilted her chin up again. "Don't you?" He bent his head and kissed her.

Her hands went to his chest and started to push him away. He started to pull back, but her right hand crept around his neck and she kissed him back. She relaxed into his arms as if she'd always fit there.

The wind intensified and she shuddered. He broke off the embrace. "Let's get you inside. You're cold."

She shook her head. "I do love you, Isaac. I love your goodness, your unwavering kindness to your friends, everything about you." She gave a choked sob and wound her arms around his neck as she kissed him again.

Even the biting wind couldn't chill him with her arms around him. When Isaac finally drew back, he was trembling. "Does this mean you'll marry me?"

Fear fluttered through her eyes. "I must explain something to you."

He tugged her cloak closer to her neck. "It can wait. I love you no matter what." He put an arm around her and led her back toward Jacob's quarters. "Let's go tell everyone."

Amelia's kitchen bustled with activity when they arrived. Morning Song was cutting up venison while Sarah peeled potatoes. Rand and Joel were putting the bread and butter out and setting the table.

Hands clasped, Emmie and Isaac stood and watched for a few moments before Sarah looked up and saw them.

"Oh. What's happened? You look so—" She broke off as she ran out of words.

"I've finally worn down Emmie's resistance," Isaac said. "She's going to be Mrs. Lieutenant Liddle."

Sarah shrieked and dropped her potatoes on the floor. She flung her arms around Emmie and danced her around the room. "I just knew you two were meant for each other," she crowed.

Rand slapped Isaac on the back and grinned. "I told you to keep trying."

Sarah gaped at her husband, then scowled at him. "You told me to stay out of it, and here I find you were the one doing the meddling."

Isaac slipped his hand around Emmie's waist. "He thought one meddling Campbell was enough."

Morning Song kissed Emmie on the cheek. "I am happy for my sister. I pray the Lord's blessings upon your life."

Emmie was touched. "Thank you, Morning Song."

Did she dare to be happy in this moment? Isaac still didn't know the full truth. While she believed his love was strong, it would take a special man to overlook the circumstances of her pregnancy. She glanced at him from the corner of her eye. He really was most remarkable. If any man could forgive her, it would be Isaac.

Joel gave a disgusted shake of his head, then shook Isaac's hand. "I guess that means another dumb wedding."

Isaac ruffled his hair and grinned. "You won't think it's so dumb in a few years."

Rand gestured to the table and chairs. "When's the wedding?"

Emmie took a seat at the table and looked hesitantly at Isaac. "We haven't discussed it yet."

"Soon," Isaac said. "I'll talk to the chaplain. How long will it take you to get ready?"

Emmie bit her lip and raised a brow in Sarah's direction. "How long?"

"A month, at least," Sarah said. "We have to make you a dress and get the food ready."

"How about we plan it for January seventeenth?"

"Make it the eleventh. That's my birthday," Rand interrupted. "I'll give her away, and I'll be giving *you* a gift on my birthday. You couldn't ask for a better gift than a new wife."

Her head reeling from the speed of everything, Emmie nodded. As they cleaned up after supper and made plans, she felt as though it was all happening to someone else. She couldn't be this happy. It wasn't possible. She kept stealing glances at Isaac's profile in the parlor, where he talked with Rand.

But what if Isaac didn't believe her about Monroe? What if he thought she had deceived him? Her mouth went dry. She had to tell him soon. She suddenly remembered Jessica. What would her reaction be? Would she really tell Isaac her perverted version of the so-called marriage? She must tell him tomorrow.

But her heart quailed at the thought. Jessica was so believable. She'd put a nasty twist on everything. Emmie would fight for him if she had to. He wasn't a man to break a promise the way Monroe had. He was worth fighting for.

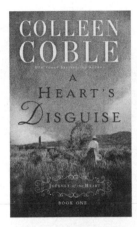
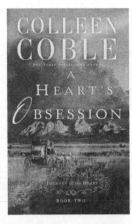
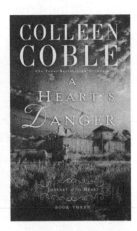
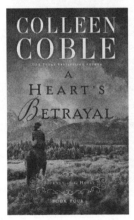
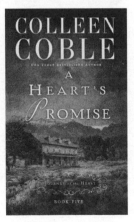
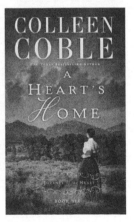

A vacation to Sunset Cove was her way of celebrating and thanking her parents. After all, Claire Dellamore's childhood was like a fairytale. But with the help of Luke Elwell, Claire discovers that fairytale was really an elaborate lie . . .

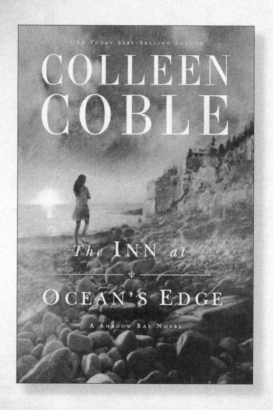

The First Sunset Cove Novel

Available in print and e-book

Thomas Nelson
Since 1798

9780718001759-B

COLLEEN LOVES TO HEAR FROM HER READERS!

Be sure to sign up for Colleen's newsletter for insider information on deals and appearances.

Visit her website at www.colleencoble.com
Twitter: @colleencoble
Facebook: colleencoblebooks

THOMAS NELSON
Since 1798

ABOUT THE AUTHOR

Photo by Clik Chick Photography

RITA finalist Colleen Coble is the author of several bestselling romantic suspense novels, including *Tidewater Inn*, and the Mercy Falls, Lonestar, and Rock Harbor series.